PEOPLE

In many ways the saying "know thyself" is not well said.
It were more practical to say "know other people!"

Menander, 343-292. Greek poet.

Other books by Peter Spier:

THE FOX WENT OUT ON A CHILLY NIGHT
PETER SPIER'S MOTHER GOOSE LIBRARY
   LONDON BRIDGE IS FALLING DOWN!
   TO MARKET! TO MARKET!
   HURRAH, WE'RE OUTWARD BOUND!
   AND SO MY GARDEN GROWS
THE ERIE CANAL
GOBBLE, GROWL, GRUNT
CRASH! BANG! BOOM!
FAST-SLOW, HIGH-LOW
THE STAR-SPANGLED BANNER
TIN-LIZZIE
NOAH'S ARK
OH, WERE THEY EVER HAPPY!
BORED—NOTHING TO DO!
PETER SPIER'S RAIN
PETER SPIER'S CHRISTMAS
THE BOOK OF JONAH
DREAMS
WE THE PEOPLE
PETER SPIER'S ADVENT CALENDAR

PEOPLE

Written and illustrated by Peter Spier

A Doubleday Book for Young Readers
Bantam Doubleday Dell Publishing Group, Inc.
1540 Broadway, New York, New York 10036

Doubleday and the portrayal of an anchor with a dolphin are trademarks of Bantam Doubleday Dell
Publishing Group, Inc.

42 43 44 45

ISBN: 0-385-13181-X Trade   0-385-13182-8 Prebound   0-385-24469-X Paperback
Library of Congress Catalog Card Number 78-19832
Summary: Emphasizes the differences among the four billion people on earth.
1. Individuality—Juvenile Literature. 2. Personality—Juvenile literature. 3. Culture—Juvenile
literature.
[1. Individuality. 2. Population]   I. Title   BF697.S68   155.2

We all know that there are lots and lots of people in the world—and many more millions each year.

There are now over 7,000,000,000 human beings on earth, and if it takes you an hour to finish looking at this book, there will be over 16,000 more!

By the year 2050 there will be 9,600,000,000 people on earth. If we all joined hands, the line would be 6,000,000 miles long and would stretch 241 times around the equator.

Or twenty-five times the distance to the moon. More than 7,000,000,000 people…and no two of them alike!

Each and every one of us different from all the others.

Each one a unique individual in his or her own right.

We come in all sizes and shapes: tall, short, and in between.

But without a single exception, we all began quite small!

And we come in many colors.

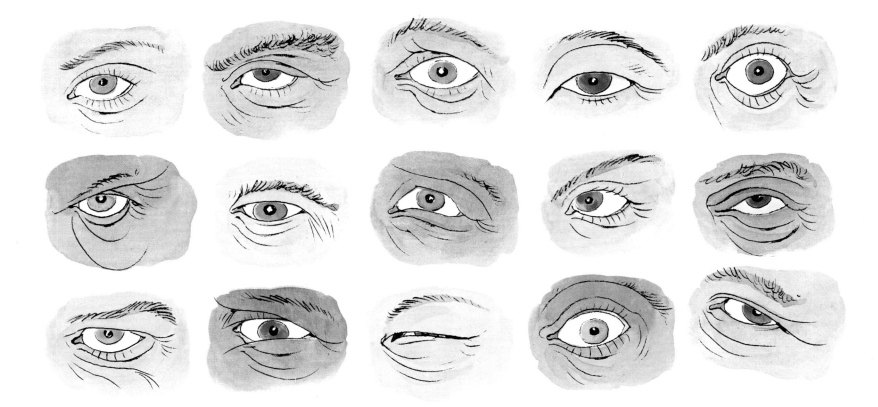

Even our eyes have different shapes and colors.

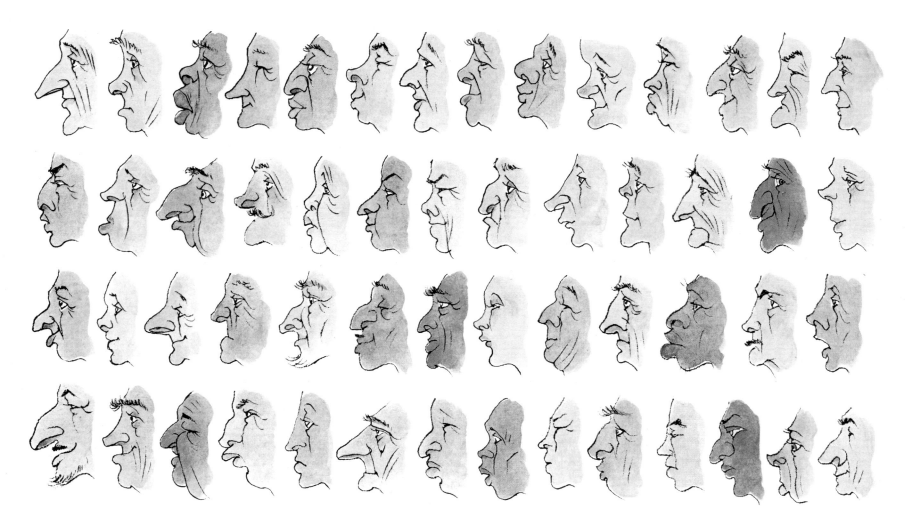

And noses come in every shape imaginable.

So do faces, lips, and ears...and everything else!

Think of our hair: from snow white to pitch black...straight, curly, kinky, and wavy. And a lot of people have no hair at all!

People are funny: Some with straight hair want theirs to be wavy, and others with little curls want theirs straight.

China Sri Lanka Britain Bantu, Africa India Schaumburg, Germany Caucasus

Normandy, France American Indian Sumatra Iraq Japan

Peru Scotland Kurdistan Swiss Guard, Vatican City Turkey Eskimo Indian, Brazil Tibet

Pakistan Papua New Guinea Lapland Java Nigeria Burma

People around our world wear different clothes— or none at all.

All of us want to look our best. Still, what is considered beautiful or handsome in one place is considered ugly, and even ridiculous, elsewhere.

Some of us are wise. Some of us are foolish. But most of us are somewhere in between.

Most people are decent, honest, friendly, and well meaning, but some are none of these.

Some of us love noise, whereas others simply cannot stand it!

And not everybody's idea of a good time is alike.

CABER TOSSING, Highland Games:
Scotland

KITE FIGHTING: S.E. Asia

PELOTE BASQUE: France

PACHISI: India's "National Game"

YOTÉ, played in holes in the ground:
West Africa

GO, the world's oldest known game:
China

HORSESHOE PITCHING: U.S.A.

CRICKET: British Isles and
Commonwealth

MURGE INLARAI, "The Cock
Fight": India

COCK FIGHTING: Indonesia

ROULETTE, a game of chance played
the world over

BOCCE: Italy. Already played by ancient
Greeks and Romans

BILBOQUET: Eskimo game of skill

OLD LADY-OLD LADY, a catching game: Pakistan

DARTS: originated in England

FISH FIGHTING: Thailand

CAMEL RUSH: Rajasthan, India

STRING FIGURES: all over Africa

YOBIZUMO, thumb wrestling: Japan

WARI, a game of skill: Africa and Arabia

SHOGI: Japanese chess

RODEO: U.S.A.

PULLING GAME: Afghanistan

SUKATAN, a starting game: Philippines

People everywhere love to play. But not the same games everywhere.

Our tastes are as different as day is from night....

Village, Syria

Rice Barge, China

Indian Long House, Brazil

Venice, Italy

in back: Village House
in front: Jhuggi, India

Papua New Guinea

Sumatra, Indonesia

Tepees, U.S.A.

Cottage, Ireland

Houseboat, Holland

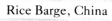

Cliffdwelling, Turkey

Mobile Home, U.S.A.

Cottage, England

Reed House, Bolivia

Eskimo Igloo, Arctic

Aborigine Dwellings, Australia

Scandinavia

Castle, England

Sudan, Africa

Camp Trailer

Cottages, Japan

Bedouin Tent, Arabia

Chad, Africa

Modern Home

Switzerland

The homes we build are as varied as we are. But we all need a roof over our heads.

What makes some people laugh makes others cry.

Some of us excel at things others could never do.

Many of us like doing things with others, while some like being by themselves.

We love and keep all sorts of pets.

Dogs, Cats, Ram, Llama, Pony, Parrots, Donkey, Rabbits, Goat, Rat, Fish, Crow

Armadillos

Mice, Gerbils, Hamsters

Birds

Crickets

Ants

Kinkajou, Coati

Turtle

Garter Snake

Frogs

Monkeys

Chameleon

Peacock

Gecko

Skunk

Celebration of Perahera. Ceylon

Befana. Italy

Thanksgiving. U.S.A.

Bastille Day. France

St. Lucia's Day. Sweden

Kanto Matsuri, Harvest Festival. Japan

Hanukkah.

Chinese New Year

Queen's Birthday. England

Feast of St. Nicholas. Holland

Moga Feast. New Guinea

Christmas

And we celebrate different feasts and holidays.

And the things we like to eat are not the same.

Eskimos: Blubber

New Guinea: Snake and Lizard

Holland: Raw Herring

Bataks, Sumatra: Dog

Africa: Elephant

Caribbean: Seaturtle

France: Froglegs and Snails

South America: Monkey

What people in one place consider a delicacy others would never touch, let alone eat!

And the foods some people eat or drink are forbidden to others.

Christians: 1,974,181,000

Jews: 14,313,000

Muslims: 1,155,109,000

Hindus: 799,028,000

Buddhists: 356,270,000

Shintoists: 2,778,000

Confucians: 6,253,000

Sikhs: 22,837,000

Taoists: 30,000,000

We practice nine main religions—and there are thousands of others as well.

God of Luck, Japan

Brahmin God of the Dance, India

Chinese God of Longevity

Hindu Goddess of the Ganges, India

Deity, New Hebrides

Madonna and Infant Jesus, Europe

Goddess of the Moon, China

Yoruba Storm God, Nigeria

The Great Goddess Devi, India

God of the Winds, Japan

Brahma the Creator, India

Hindu Snake God, Ceylon

Buddhist God of Wisdom, India

Hindu God of War, India

Thou shalt make thee no molten gods. Exodus, 34:17

Sea God, Nigeria

Sun Worshippers, Asia

Deity, New Guinea

God of Wealth, China

Many people believe in one God…and millions of others believe in many gods. And many millions more do not believe in anything at all.

Most of us have to work for a living, and there are more different ways of doing that than you would believe.

Matador

Soldier

Teapicker

Gondolier

Circus Clown

Snake Charmer

Fortune Teller

Museum Guard

Inventor

Diver

Astronaut

Cheese Porter

Opera Singer

Riksha Driver

Archaeologist

Paper Vendor, Police Officer, Window Washer, Balloon Vendor, Letter Carrier, Streetsweeper, Chimneysweep, Fruitseller, Telephone Lineworker, Deliveryman, Garbage Collector, Fire Fighter, Beggar, Street Musician

Most people work hard, but others are lazy. And a lot of people who want to work, cannot find a job!

And some of us are rich, although most are not.
And very many are desperately poor.

Almost everybody can speak. But there are 201
different main languages spoken on earth...not
to mention the countless variants and dialects
spoken by smaller groups.

Signal Flags

Telephones and
Communication Satellites

Tom-tom

Television

Wireless, Morse Code

Semaphore Flags

Signalling Lamp

Records and Cassette

Walkie-talkies

And deaf people can communicate in silence—through sign language!

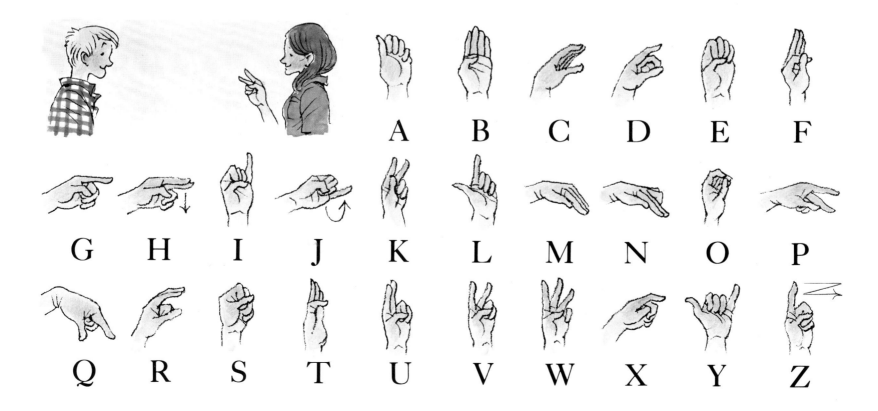

A B C D E F

G H I J K L M N O P

Q R S T U V W X Y Z

Die ganze neuere Geschichte,
dem Anscheine nach ein Triumphzug

Gothic

παντοίων ἀγαθῶν, ἅπερ
ΑΒΓΔ ΞΟΠΡΣΤΥΦΧΨΩ

Greek

beaċa ṁaṗċanaċ aige.

Gaelic

Інсоуса имѫть льстинѫ и

Cyrillic

Французская литература

Russian

Երբ այսպէս ամեն

Armenian

მაშინ პირჯვარს დაიწერსა:

Georgian

ⲠⲈⲚⲈⲒⲰⲦ ⲈⲦ ϦⲚ̅Ⲙ̅ⲠⲎⲨⲈ

Coptic

וַיֹּאמֶר אֱלֹהִים יְהִי־אוֹר וַיְהִי־אוֹר׃

Hebrew

مُلْكِهِ فَرَأَى رَهْجًا قَرِيبًا مِنْهُ فَقَا

Arabic

هكذا افول لكم

Arabic (Tunisia)

آه هلک نه هوئے سگوں

Arabic (Persian)

እስመ ፡ ከመዝ ፡ አፍቀሮ ፡

Ethiopic

[illegible]

Syriac (Estrangelo)

[illegible]

Syriac (Serto)

[illegible]

Pahlavi

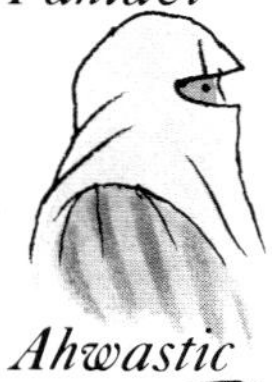

[illegible]

Ahwastic

यत ईश्वरो जगतीत्थं प्रेम

Devanagari

আমি তোমাদিগকে বলিতেছি,

Bengali

કેમકે ખોદાએ દુનીઆ

Gujarati

མི་སྲུ་དེ་ཀི་རྗེ་ཀོན་ཆོག་གི་ཁྲུག་ཆད་

Tibetan

தேவன் தம்முடைய ஒரேபேறான

Tamil

ఆలానే మతి ఊతాని

Telugu

ದೇವರು ಲೋಕದ ಮೇಲೆ ಎಷ್ಟೋ

Kanarese

Malayalam തനെറ ഏകജാതനായ

Singhalese එපමණ ප්‍රෙමකළෙසේක.

Thai นั้น จะ ฆิ ได้ ฉิบหาย,

Burmese ကသွ္ာတံသ္ဒွဟ္ဒှ်ာ သင္ဌ

Javanese ꦱꦺꦏ꧀ꦫꦒꦻꦴꦲꦾꦴꦩꦸꦲꦶꦥꦸꦴ

Balinese ꦮꦴꦴ ꦲꦶ ꦤꦸꦲꦶꦩꦶ

Vietnamese Ẳ Ẳ Ặ Ẫ Ấ Ầ Ẩ Ẵ Ậ Đ É È Ẻ Ẽ Ẹ Ê É
Í Ì Ỉ Ị Ó Ò Ỏ Õ Ọ Ủ Ũ Ụ Ý Ỳ Ỷ Ỹ Ỵ

Cherokee Ꮣ Ꮑ Ꮧ Ꮛ Ꮰ Ꮲ Ꮴ Ꮖ Ꮺ Ꮼ Ꮚ Ꮬ Ꮁ Ꮮ
Ꮐ Ꮙ Ꭰ Ꮳ Ꮝ Ꮞ Ꮯ Ꭲ Ꮻ Ꮵ Ꮷ Ꮿ Ꮎ Ꮈ

Chinese

Chinese (Wang-ts joa)

Korean

Manchu

Mongolian

Kalmuck

Japanese (Katakana)

Japanese (Hiragana)

Not nearly all the world's people can read and
write, yet there are almost one hundred different
ways of doing it.

Some people, but very few, are mighty and
powerful, although most of us are not mighty at all.

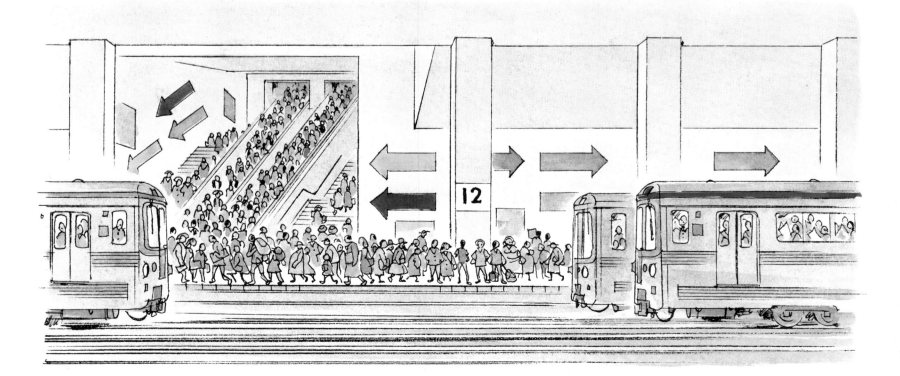

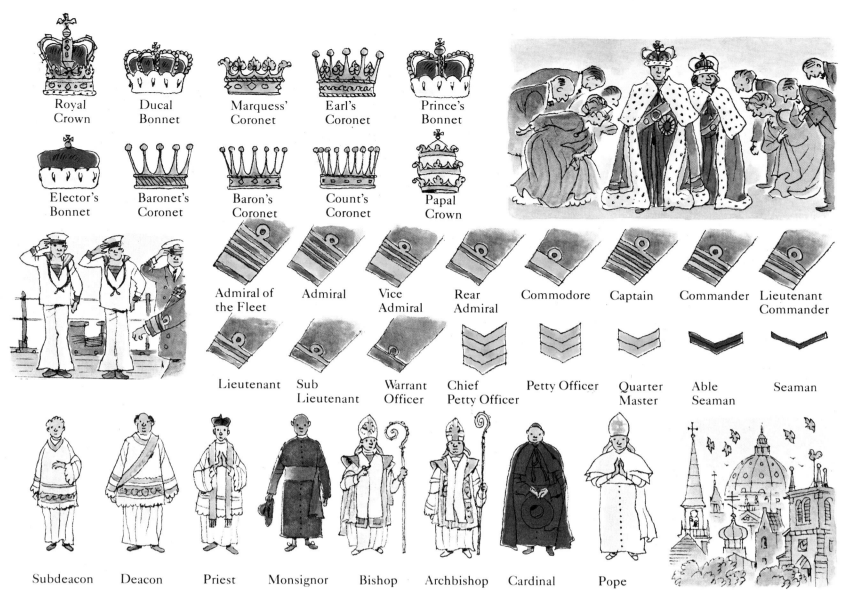

Royal Crown · Ducal Bonnet · Marquess' Coronet · Earl's Coronet · Prince's Bonnet

Elector's Bonnet · Baronet's Coronet · Baron's Coronet · Count's Coronet · Papal Crown

Admiral of the Fleet · Admiral · Vice Admiral · Rear Admiral · Commodore · Captain · Commander · Lieutenant Commander

Lieutenant · Sub Lieutenant · Warrant Officer · Chief Petty Officer · Petty Officer · Quarter Master · Able Seaman · Seaman

Subdeacon · Deacon · Priest · Monsignor · Bishop · Archbishop · Cardinal · Pope

We have invented a strange system of ranks, grades, and classes…

Yet we all live on the same planet, breathe the same air, and warm ourselves in the same sun.

And in the end we all must die.

Pyramid of Cheops, Egypt
Cheops, c.2680BC, Pharao

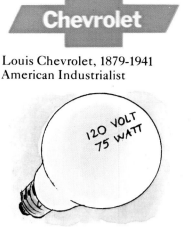

Chevrolet

Louis Chevrolet, 1879-1941
American Industrialist

Alessandro Volta, 1745-1827,
Italian Physicist
James Watt, 1736-1819,
Scottish Inventor

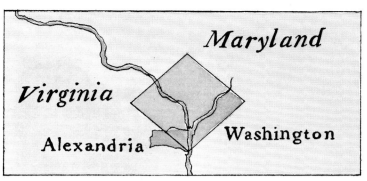

Henrietta Maria, 1609-1669, Queen of England
George Washington, 1732 -1799, General and Pres. U.S.
John Alexander, 18th C. American Landowner
Virginia: Elizabeth I, 1533-1603, Queen of England

James Chapman, 19th C.
British Discoverer

Augustus, 63BC-AD14
Roman Emperor

Winston S. Churchill 1874-1965
British Statesman, Author

George F. Handel, 1685-1759,
English Composer

Martin Luther, 1483-1546,
German Reformer

George II, 1683-1760,
King of Great Britain

Mohandas K. Gandhi,
1869-1948
Indian Nationalist Leader

Ludwig van Beethoven, 1770-1827, German Composer

John F. Kennedy, 1917-1963,
President of the U S.

Bartolomeo Colleoni, 1400-1475,
Italian Soldier of Fortune

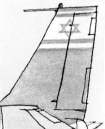

Star of David
David, d.972BC,
Hebrew King

Trampoline: Mr. du Trampolin,
Medieval French Acrobat

Wilhelmina, 1880-1962, Queen of the Netherlands

Sir Thomas Lipton, 1850-1931
Scottish Merchant

Nelson's Column, London
Viscount Horatio Nelson, 1753-1805
English Admiral

Gardenia:
Alexander Garden, d.1791,
Scottish Naturalist

Pierre Corneille, 1606-1684, French Dramatist

Jesus Christ, d.33AD

Nero, AD37-68
Roman Emperor

Mount Everest, Nepal -Tibet
Sir George Everest, 1790-1866,
British Surveyor

Benjamin Franklin, 1706-1790
American Statesman, Scientist

Louis Pasteur, 1822-1895,
French Chemist

Hon. C.S. Rolls, 1877-1910,
British Manufacturer
Sir F.H. Royce, 1863-1933,
British Engineer

Guillotine: Dr. Guillotin,
b.1738, French Physician

Rudolph Diesel, 1858-1913
German Engineer

Adelie Penguin.
Adelie d'Urville,
Wife of 19th C.
French Explorer

Louis Quinze Table
Louis XV, 1710-1774,
French King

St. Valentine, c.270,
Roman Martyr Priest

William Shakespeare, 1564-1616,
English Dramatist
Richard II , 1452-1485,
King of England

Christopher Columbus, 1451-1506,
Italian-Spanish Discoverer

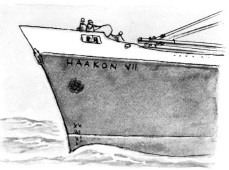

Haakon VII, 1872-1957,
King of Norway

A few of us are remembered long, long after
we're gone. And even that, in countless different
ways!

Seven billion human beings…young and old, sick and well, happy and unhappy, kind and unkind, strong and weak.

People everywhere.
And all different.

It is very strange: Some people even hate others because they are unlike themselves. Because they are different. They forget that they too would seem different if they could only see themselves through other people's eyes.

But imagine how dreadfully dull this world of ours would be if everybody looked, thought, ate, dressed, and acted the same!

Now, isn't it wonderful that each and every one of us is unlike any other?